Louanne Pig in
The Perfect
Family

Louanne Pig in The Perfect Family

NANCY CARLSON

Carolrhoda Books, Inc. / Minneapolis

This book is available in two editions:
Library binding by Carolrhoda Books, Inc., a division of Lerner Publishing Group
Soft cover by First Avenue Editions, an imprint of Lerner Publishing Group
241 First Avenue North
Minneapolis, MN 55401 U.S.A.

Website address: www.lernerbooks.com

Library of Congress Cataloging-in-Publication Data

Carlson, Nancy L.
      Louanne Pig in the perfect family / written and illustrated by Nancy Carlson.
          p.   cm.
      Summary: Louanne thinks she wants to be part of a big family until she spends a weekend with her friend George and his five sisters and four brothers..
      ISBN: 1–57505–611–9 (lib. bdg. : alk. paper)
      ISBN: 1–57505–616–X (pbk. : alk. paper)
      [1. Brothers and sisters—Fiction. 2. Family life—Fiction. 3. Pigs—Fiction.] I. Title.
      PZ7.C21665Lo 2004
      [E]—dc21   2003004148

Manufactured in the United States of America
1 2 3 4 5 6 – JR – 09 08 07 06 05 04

To my perfect family,
Barry and Kelly

Louanne lived with her mother and her father. George lived next door with his mother and his father and his five sisters and his four brothers. There was never a dull moment in *their* yard.

"Don't you think ten kids make a perfect family?" Louanne asked her mom.

"You and Daddy are the perfect family for me," said Mom.

"Didn't you ever think about adopting some more kids?" Louanne asked her dad.

"Nope," said Dad. "You're all I can handle."

Then one night Mom said, "My office just called. I have to fly to Dallas in the morning, and this is Daddy's fishing weekend. How would you like to spend the weekend at George's house?"

"Would I ever!" said Louanne.

On Friday afternoon, Louanne packed two nice outfits, a nightgown, a good book, her toothbrush and toothpaste, a towel, and a large bag of jelly beans.

"Off I go!" she told her parents.

"I'm afraid you'll have to share a bedroom with the girls," George's mother told Louanne.

"Oh, that will be wonderful," said Louanne. "I've never shared a room before."

George took Louanne upstairs so she could leave her suitcase in her room. Then they went outside to play.

As they ran outside, Louanne slipped on a roller skate and fell down.

"You have to watch your step around here," said George. "Hal leaves his stuff all over the place."

In the middle of a game of catch, Louanne felt her shirt getting wet.

"Is it raining?" she asked.

"No, it's Tony," said George. "He got a new squirt gun this morning. Just ignore him, and he'll go away."

Suddenly a loud bell began to clang.

"Dinner!" yelled George, and Louanne was left behind in a cloud of dust.

By the time she made it to the table, everyone
else was already there.

"Hey, Margaret, pass the corn before you've
taken it all!" Tony was yelling.

"Tony," wailed Harry, "you took the last carrot!"

"Pass the squash!" yelled Hal.

"*Please* pass the squash," said his mother.

"ME FIRST!" yelled Hal.

Dinner at my house is never like this, thought Louanne.

Later Louanne went upstairs to unpack. Her clothes were strewn all over the room, and her bag of jelly beans was nearly empty.

"It must have been Nancy," said George. "She gets into everything. She's too little to know better."

That night Louanne made an even worse discovery: Eleanor snored.

The next morning Louanne didn't feel too rested. Maybe a cold shower will wake me up, she thought, but she was last in line for the bathroom.

At breakfast George's mother announced a picnic
in the park. Oh, good, thought Louanne. Maybe
George and I can sneak away and play by ourselves.

But George had to help keep an eye on the little kids,

and the potato salad wasn't the way Louanne's
mother made it, either.

That evening Louanne tried to find a quiet
corner where she could read, but it was no use.

"Doesn't all this noise all the time drive you crazy?" she asked George.

George looked surprised. "I like it this way," he said.

Sunday morning Louanne packed her suitcase again. As soon as she saw her parents drive up, she rushed home.

"Boy, am I glad to see you!" said Louanne.
"How was your weekend?" Mom asked. "Was
it fun being part of a big family?"
"Oh, a big family is just great—for George."

"But you and Daddy are the perfect family for me. Do we have any more jelly beans?"